Silver Dolphins

STORMY SKIES

Dorset Libraries
Withdrawn Stock

*For the Troths, Dianne, Richard,
Eleanor and Isabel*

www.summerwaters.co.uk

First published in paperback by HarperCollins *Children's Books* in 2010

HarperCollins *Children's Books* is a division of HarperCollins *Publishers* Ltd,
77-85 Fulham Palace Road, Hammersmith, London W6 8JB.

Visit our website at: www.harpercollins.co.uk

1 3 5 7 9 10 8 6 4 2
ISBN-13: 978-0-00-734813-8

A CIP catalogue record for this title is available from the British Library.
All rights reserved.

Typeset by Palimpsest Book Production Limited,
Grangemouth, Stirlingshire

Printed and bound in England by Clays Ltd, St Ives plc

Mixed Sources
Product group from well-managed
forests and other controlled sources
www.fsc.org Cert no. SW-COC-1806
© 1996 Forest Stewardship Council

FSC is a non-profit international organisation established to promote the
responsible management of the world's forests. Products carrying the FSC
label are independently certified to assure consumers that they come
from forests that are managed to meet the social, economic and
ecological needs of present and future generations.

Find out more about HarperCollins and the environment at
www.harpercollins.co.uk/green

by Summer Waters

Silver Dolphins

STORMY SKIES

HarperCollins *Children's Books*

Prologue

A small dolphin was tugging at a piece of seaweed half buried under a rock. It was the longest piece he'd ever seen and just right for a game of seaweed tag.

"Hurry up, Bubbles," called his sister Dream. "Any piece of seaweed will do. It doesn't have to be that bit."

"It does," clicked Bubbles, scraping away at the sand. "This bit's perfect. Come and help me dig it out."

Dream sighed, but to speed the game up she swam over to help her brother, digging up the sand with her nose.

"It's nearly out," grunted Bubbles.

He tugged harder until, in a sudden flurry of sand, the seaweed came free. Bubbles jerked backwards, spinning into Dream, who then crashed into their friend Phantom.

"Ouch!" squeaked Phantom, falling into the path of Spirit and Star.

"Watch out!" clicked Spirit, but it was too late. The dolphins bumped heavily into each other.

"Help!" whistled Star, who was squashed between the two of them.

Bubbles righted himself then swam over to help his mum.

"Thank you," she clicked, flexing her bruised tail.

"Sorry, Mum." Bubbles hung his head in shame. "I didn't mean to hurt anyone."

"I know you didn't," clicked Star kindly. "You weren't thinking. Next time maybe you will."

A cold feeling came over Spirit. The oceans were suffering because people didn't stop to think about their actions either. It was lucky they had the Silver Dolphins. They had made a huge difference to sea life. Spirit sensed greater challenges lay ahead, but knew they would do their best to meet them. With every new challenge the Silver Dolphins grew stronger.

The thought warmed him.

Chapter One

Antonia waved goodbye to her mum then closed the front door. She turned to her friend Hannah Davies and said excitedly, "I can't believe we're actually here. We've been counting the days, haven't we, Cai?"

"You bet," said Cai. "It seems like ages since we last saw you."

It was the half-term holiday and Antonia and Cai were staying with Hannah for a few days.

"I can't believe it either," said Hannah. "It's going to be great. Come on. I'll show you your rooms. This is yours, Cai."

She opened a door on to an airy room with a small double bed, wardrobe and a chest of drawers. "Antonia's sharing with me."

"Cool," said Cai, dumping his bag on the floor.

"My room's got a balcony, so if you stand by the rail, you can just see the sea through the trees," said Hannah, leading the way out of Cai's room and across the hall. She threw open a door, revealing a pretty room with blue walls and an enormous metal bunk bed. "You can have the top bed if you like, Antonia."

"Thanks. This is a great room, Hannah. You've got loads of stuff." Antonia stared at the flat-screen television, mini sound system and shelves bulging with books and trinkets.

Hannah blushed. "That's Mum's fault. She buys me things to make up for hardly ever being around. I can't believe she's managed to arrange to work from home this week. She's so busy at the moment. I told her she didn't need to as we'd be spending our time helping Kathleen, but she insisted."

"I can't wait to meet Kathleen," said Antonia. Her fingers strayed to the silver dolphin charm she always wore round her neck.

Antonia, Cai and Hannah shared a magical secret. They were Silver Dolphins, guardians of the sea. This meant that they had special

magical abilities that allowed them to swim and communicate with real dolphins so they could look after the ocean and the creatures living there. Silver Dolphins were rare; only someone who believed in magic and was in tune with nature could be one.

Cai's great aunty Claudia had been a Silver Dolphin once, but now she ran a marine conservation charity called Sea Watch. Kathleen, a friend of Hannah's mum, had also been a Silver Dolphin and Antonia and Cai were staying with Hannah to help Kathleen set up her own marine conservation charity.

"Kathleen can't wait to meet you too," said Hannah. "You should see her new house. It's got a huge garden overlooking the estuary. It's the perfect place for a marine charity. Did I

tell you she's decided to call it Ocean Watch to avoid confusion with Sea Watch?"

"Ocean Watch." Antonia tried the name out. "I like it."

"Me too," said Cai. "When do we get to meet Kathleen?"

"Tomorrow. Mum's taking us out for tea now. She's hopeless at cooking. We're going to a little café at the top of the cliffs. It does great food and the views are amazing. You can often see dolphins in the sea. We used to go there all the time, but we haven't been for ages. I hope they still do their lasagne. It's the best ever."

"Let's go then," said Cai, who was always hungry. Antonia and Hannah laughed.

"I'll go and see if Mum's ready," said Hannah.

"It gets dark really early these days. If we don't go soon, we won't be able to see the view."

Lottie Davies, Hannah's mum, was in her bedroom working on the computer.

"Have a look at these, Han," she said when Hannah knocked on her door. "They're the photos I took for that new clothes range. What do you think?"

"Nice," said Hannah politely. "Can we go out for tea now?"

Mrs Davies glanced at the clock on her computer. "Goodness! Is that the time?" she exclaimed. "You must be starving. Let me just email these pictures to work and I'll be right with you. Go and get the car keys, Hannah. They're in the kitchen drawer."

Hannah and her mum lived in the first-floor apartment of a smart block of flats. While her mum sent her email and shut down the computer, Hannah collected the car keys then took Antonia and Cai outside to show them the shared gardens.

"There's a gate at the bottom that leads to a public footpath. If you follow it all the way down, it comes out at the beach," said Hannah. "I can get to the sea within five minutes of Vision's call."

Antonia felt a shiver of excitement. Vision was the leader of the dolphin pod that Hannah swam with and he knew Antonia and Cai's dolphin leader, Spirit. Antonia was longing to meet him.

The café was a short drive from Hannah's

apartment; dusk was already beginning to fall as Mrs Davies drove her car up the winding road to the cliff top. In the front passenger seat Hannah eagerly craned forward as the car pulled into a large car park.

"Here it is—" Hannah broke off suddenly. "But it's shut!"

"Hop out and see when it opens," said Mrs Davies, switching off the engine.

Pushing her long blonde hair over her shoulder, Antonia climbed out of the car and followed Hannah across the car park to the café. She passed a rusty litter bin surrounded by weeds and a wooden bench with broken legs. Antonia shivered. This place had a sad, empty feel to it.

"It's closed down," wailed Hannah, who'd

reached the café first and was peering through the window. "There's nothing here."

Cai pointed to a large sign mounted on the corner of the building. "It's for sale," he read. "Cliff-top café with parking; includes three acres of land with planning permission for twelve houses."

"More houses!" exclaimed Hannah. "There won't be any countryside left around here soon."

"It's a fantastic location," said Cai, making his way round the side of the café until he was standing at the back of the building. "Come and look at this view."

"Oh, no!" Hannah gasped in dismay. "Look what they've done! They've chopped all the trees down. You can see even further now.

I never knew there was a cove down there. And what's that on the beach?"

"Seals," said Antonia. "A whole colony. Can we go down for a closer look?"

"We can't from up here. There's no path," Hannah answered.

As Antonia stepped forward for a better look at the seals, a strange sensation swept over her. She froze, her hand lightly covering her silver dolphin charm as she waited for the call of the dolphins. But there was no sound in Antonia's head and the dolphin charm, with its silky-soft body, lay silently against her neck. Antonia's skin prickled with foreboding.

"Whoa!" cried Cai, reaching out and catching hold of her arm. "Don't go any further.

It's not safe. Look how the ground is crumbling away."

"Thanks, but I wasn't going to," said Antonia. "I bet that's happened since the trees got chopped down. Tree roots hold the soil together and stop erosion."

"We're learning about that in geography," said Hannah. "I've even got holiday homework on it. I should get Mum to come and take some photos for me. Not now though – I'm starving. I can't believe this place has closed, especially as all the outside tables and benches are still here. I hope someone buys it quickly and opens it up again."

Disappointed, she headed back to the car. Cai followed, but Antonia hung back for a moment, apprehensively watching the seals

on the beach. There were so many of them in such a small space. Although it was getting difficult to see in the fading light, Antonia spotted some seal pups. They were very sweet, all snuggled up with the adults. Antonia grinned to herself. She was being silly. There was nothing to worry about here, except where to go for tea now the café had closed down!

Chapter Two

Darkness was just beginning to lift when Antonia woke. Sleepily she opened her eyes, wondering why her room felt different. Then she remembered. She was staying at Hannah's. She sat up as a familiar sensation nudged her fully awake. The dolphins were going to call. Hurriedly she

swung her legs over the side of the bunk
and climbed down the ladder. As she reached
the floor, her dolphin charm began to vibrate
and an unfamiliar voice sounded in her
head.

Silver Dolphin, we need you.

Vision, I hear your call, Antonia silently
answered, guessing it must be the dolphin
leader. His voice was higher than Spirit's and
he spoke more quickly.

Antonia searched for her clothes, rummaging
in the drawer that Hannah had emptied for her
the night before. It was difficult to see clearly,
but she didn't switch the light on. Antonia's
silver dolphin charm fluttered against her neck.
As it began to beat with a steady rhythm, the
charm emitted a high-pitched whistle. Hannah's

charm whistled too, waking her. She jumped out of bed in a flash.

"You heard first?" she asked as she pulled on a pair of grey cargo trousers hanging from a chair.

Flushing with embarrassment, Antonia nodded. She didn't want Hannah to think she was showing off, but Hannah grinned, happy to accept that Antonia was a more powerful Silver Dolphin than her. They finished dressing in silence and crept into the hall, meeting up there with Cai, who came out of his room carrying his shoes.

"Let's go," whispered Hannah, unbolting the front door.

"What about writing a note for your mum?" Antonia reminded her.

"No need," said Hannah. "Mum's used to me doing my own thing. And it's Sunday. She never gets up this early!"

Hannah closed the front door of the flat and led the way along the corridor, down the stairs and across the lobby to the apartment's communal front door. Even though only a Silver Dolphin could hear the call, the shrill whistle still made Antonia nervous. Wincing, she followed Hannah outside. The grass was heavy with dew and by the time they reached the gate at the end of the garden, Antonia's trainers were soaked.

Hannah pelted down the public footpath, Antonia and Cai hot on her heels running side by side. Soon the ground began to level out, and as the trees thinned, Antonia caught the

smell of the sea. She inhaled deeply, loving its sharp, salty tang and the mewling cries of the early morning gulls.

The path ended in a kissing gate. One by one the Silver Dolphins squeezed through it. Hannah didn't wait for Antonia and Cai, but sprinted up the sand dunes rising before her.

Antonia followed, the soft sand shifting under her feet. Her calf muscles protested at the unfamiliar sensation of running uphill on moving sand. Spiky green marram grass grew everywhere and it whipped against Antonia's trousers as if urging her on. Panting with exertion, she arrived at the top of the dunes and stood there for a moment, her eyes scanning the vast expanse of sand ahead.

"Wow!" exclaimed Cai.

"It's huge," Antonia agreed. The sand spread before them like an enormous yellow canvas, the sea a splash of blue on the horizon.

"Hurry," urged Hannah, pulling off her shoes and socks.

Antonia and Cai did the same, leaving their shoes hidden in a clump of marram grass. Antonia's bare toes found it hard to grip on to the powdery dunes and she kept sliding backwards. At the bottom the sand was much firmer. Antonia pounded across the beach with Cai, catching up with Hannah and running alongside her as she raced towards the flat sea. The water was icy cold. Gritting her teeth, Antonia braced herself and dived in.

Silver Dolphin, we need you.

I'm on my way.

The shock of the freezing water made Antonia gasp out loud, but seconds later her legs melded together like a dolphin's tail and she stopped noticing the cold. She was a Silver Dolphin! Antonia whistled for joy as her body arched in and out of the steely-grey sea.

"Over there," panted Hannah after they'd been swimming for ages.

Antonia had felt the dolphins' vibrations long before she spotted their four silver heads anxiously bobbing in the water. Hannah swam towards the largest, a proud-looking common dolphin whose wise eyes were lined with stripes that ran to his mouth.

"Welcome, Silver Dolphins. Thank you for answering my call," clicked Vision. After quickly greeting everyone by rubbing noses, he clicked, "Follow me."

Chapter Three

Vision led the Silver Dolphins to a large rock rising from the sea like a jagged mountain. An animal was floundering around on top and, as the Silver Dolphins came closer, Antonia saw it was a grey seal. She swam faster, reaching the rock ahead of Cai and Hannah.

It was a struggle to clamber out of the water and up the rock's barnacle-encrusted side. Antonia's foot slipped on a strand of wet seaweed and she started to fall backwards. Cai saved her by putting his hand on her back and pushing her up again. Gratefully Antonia regained her balance on the rock and held out her hand to help Cai then Hannah up too. There wasn't much room and the seal eyed them warily, her whiskery nose quivering with alarm.

"Steady," crooned Antonia, holding out her hands palms upwards to show the seal she meant no harm.

The seal didn't move, but her grey-tan sides heaved fearfully as she breathed in and out.

"You're a big girl." Antonia spoke in a low,

calm voice as she took a step closer. The seal had an enormous belly and Antonia guessed she was carrying a pup.

"Oh!" Antonia's breath caught in her throat as she spotted a long scratch on the seal's flipper. The seal had been lucky. Something sharp had done that and it could have caused a much nastier injury.

"Here," said Hannah, pulling a small plastic pack of tissues from her pocket.

"Thanks." Antonia took them and cleaned the dirt from around the scratch. The seal flinched, but Cai and Hannah reassured her with calm words.

"There," said Antonia, putting the tissues in her pocket.

The seal seemed in no hurry to leave the

rock. She nudged each of the Silver Dolphins, her whiskery nose tickling them and making them giggle.

"Another job done," said Hannah with a grin.

"Not quite. We don't know what injured the seal. It had to be something caused by humans or pollution or we wouldn't have been called to help." Antonia peered into the sea as if the answer might be obvious.

"You're right," said Cai. "We'd better have a look around."

One at a time they lowered themselves from the rock and into the sea. Antonia was last, holding back to say goodbye to her new friend. When she finally splashed into the water, Vision had been joined by the three dolphins

Antonia had seen earlier. Hannah swam among the dolphins as she introduced them.

"This is Dancer, Vision's wife." Hannah pointed to a pretty dolphin with a rich gold blaze and dreamy eyes. Dancer bobbed forward and greeted the Silver Dolphins by patting their heads with her flipper.

"This is Lulu, Vision and Dream's daughter," Hannah continued.

Clicking a laugh, Lulu rolled in the water, flashing her silver belly at them. Then, righting herself, she squeaked, "And this is Rolly, my best friend."

"And that's Lulu's friend Rolly," said Hannah, laughing.

"Hi, Silver Dolphins," clicked Rolly, smacking the water with his fin.

"Can we play with the Silver Dolphins?" asked Lulu.

"We haven't finished yet," said Antonia. "We have to find out what scratched the seal's flipper before another animal gets hurt."

"We'll help. We're good at looking for things, aren't we, Rolly?" clicked Lulu immediately. Rolly nodded enthusiastically.

"Calm down, Lulu," clicked Vision. "You can help the Silver Dolphins, but please be careful. If you find something that shouldn't be in the sea, don't touch it. Call the Silver Dolphins to deal with it."

"Thanks, Dad." Lulu splashed her delight. "Come on, Silver Dolphins – let's go!"

Antonia, Cai and Hannah dived down to the seabed where they spread out and began

searching for the object that had injured the seal. The water was murky and for a long while no one spoke as they concentrated on the task. Cai found a length of fishing twine which he coiled up and put in his pocket. Hannah rescued a small crab from inside a discarded crisp packet and Antonia found a wad of newspaper that disintegrated as she picked it up.

"None of this injured the seal." Feeling frustrated, Antonia stuffed the bits of newspaper inside the crisp packet then shoved it into her pocket.

"We've been looking for ages and there's nothing here. Can we play now?" asked Lulu.

Antonia had one last look around. "OK, let's play Sprat."

"Bubbly!" clicked Lulu. "I'll be it. I'll give you a three waves' head start."

"I'm gone!" With a flick of his tail, Rolly swam away quickly, followed by Cai and Hannah. Antonia hesitated. If only she could find what had injured the seal, she would feel much happier. But she wanted to play Sprat with Lulu and Rolly too and they had searched the seabed for ages.

"Coming to get you," clicked Lulu.

Promising herself she'd have another look around before she went home, Antonia ducked behind a rock, then changing direction, swam away. Lulu wasn't that easily fooled. She hared after Antonia, tagging her with a flipper.

"Sprat, you're it," she whistled then darted away before Antonia could tag her back.

Antonia cruised in the water. She couldn't see anyone, but she could sense vibrations to her left. Quietly she swam towards the movement, startling Rolly, who was hiding in a bed of seaweed.

"Tag," clicked Antonia, stretching out her hand, but Rolly was too quick for her and swam away before she could touch him. Antonia gave chase, churning up the sea as she went after him.

The gap was closing when Rolly turned a somersault and veered off to the right. It was a neat move and it was a few seconds before Antonia realised what had happened. By the time she'd changed direction again, Rolly had disappeared. The water was even cloudier here and Antonia slowed as she navigated her way

along the seabed. Something large loomed before her. Cautiously Antonia swam towards it until she was close enough to see a large metal shape.

"Truce!" she clicked excitedly. "I've found what injured the seal."

Chapter Four

Immediately Cai and Lulu swam up from behind a rock. Hannah appeared from the other direction.

"What is it?" asked Lulu curiously.

"It's a metal sign," said Hannah. "People stand these outside shops to show what's inside. This one's advertising coffee. No wonder

the seal was hurt. It looks like she got her flipper caught in the bit that swings."

"How did it get here?" Antonia wondered aloud.

"Someone probably threw it into the sea for a joke. The big question is – how are we going to get it out?" asked Cai, running a hand through his dark curly hair.

"With great care," said Antonia, gingerly holding the sign's metal middle so that it couldn't swing shut and trap her fingers. "Keep back, Lulu and Rolly."

Lulu had been edging closer, but moved away as the Silver Dolphins closed in and prepared to move the sign.

"Ready?" asked Cai. "Lift."

Grunting with effort, Antonia, Cai and

Hannah swam, lifting the sign up to the surface. It was heavy and awkward to hold. They swam slowly to avoid injuring themselves. Once they surfaced, they laid the sign flat then trod water to get their breath back.

"Phew! It's heavy," Antonia panted.

Hannah was scanning the coastline with her piercing grey eyes. At last she said, "We're near the café we went to last night. If you look up, you can see where the trees have been cut down. And to the right is the beach with the seal colony. I think this sign came from that café. There used to be one exactly the same outside it."

"You're right," said Cai excitedly. "I can see the back of the café from here."

"I wonder… Do you think the sign might

have fallen off the cliff? Only the ground wasn't very safe up there," suggested Antonia.

"It might have," said Hannah. "I don't suppose we'll ever know. The important thing is not to leave it here to hurt anyone else."

"Does that mean you have to go home now? That's the shortest game of Sprat ever," grumbled Lulu.

"We'll have a longer game next time," Hannah promised her.

It was a slow swim back to the beach. Antonia's fingers ached from keeping them clamped round the sign's metal middle. Once she let go and nearly trapped her fingers. Lulu and Rolly swam alongside, clicking encouragement. When the beach came in

sight, they said goodbye, but without the usual rubbing of noses.

"We won't come any closer," said Lulu warily. "See you soon, Silver Dolphins. Dad's going to be very pleased when we tell him you've made the sea safe for us again."

"Bye, Lulu, bye, Rolly," everyone clicked back.

They trod water, watching the two dolphins swim away, their bodies a silver blur as they raced back to their pod.

"Better get this ashore," said Antonia when the dolphins were tiny specks on the horizon.

As the water grew shallower, the sign became heavier and more cumbersome to move. They paddled through the surf and up the sand, water pouring from their clothes

until they were totally dry with only their hair feeling slightly damp.

"We left our shoes over there," said Antonia, changing direction.

Panting with effort, Antonia, Cai and Hannah carried the coffee sign up the beach and stood it upright in the sand.

"What do we do with it now?" asked Cai. "We can't leave it here."

"I know," said Hannah. She smiled mischievously. "Let's take it to Kathleen – her place isn't so far from here. It'll be our first gift from the sea to Ocean Watch."

Antonia and Cai chuckled. "That's a great idea," they agreed.

Hurriedly they pulled on their socks and shoes then, turning the sign on its side to

carry it, they set out to Kathleen's. The day was getting lighter and a few early risers were out walking their dogs on the beach. A friendly Labrador ran up and sniffed at the sign until his owner called him away. She stared suspiciously at Antonia, Cai and Hannah, as if they were up to no good.

"We're cleaning up the beach," Cai called out.

The lady was surprised. "Well done," she said. "It's good to see young people behaving responsibly for a change."

"What's that supposed to mean?" asked Cai indignantly as she walked away. "Most young people *are* responsible."

"Forget it," said Antonia. "Let's get this sign to Kathleen's. Then we can go back home and have breakfast. I'm starving."

"Me too," said Hannah. "Mum should be up by now. If not, there's cereal and I can make toast."

They carried the sign over the dunes, their feet slipping and sliding in the soft sand.

"Kathleen lives this way," said Hannah, bearing left before they got to the path to her own home. They skirted round a natural harbour filled with sailing dinghies and followed the path running alongside the estuary. Several times they were forced to stop for a rest. Antonia was relieved when Hannah said, "We're nearly there."

On one side lay the estuary and on the other a row of houses with long back gardens. Almost every house had a gate that opened on to the path. Some of the gardens were open

and you could see as far as the house, but others were screened by bushes and trees. As they approached a house with a beech hedge thick with copper-coloured leaves, Hannah slowed down.

"We're here," she said, stopping at the wooden gate butting up to the hedge. She twisted the iron ring and pushed the gate open.

"Wow!" exclaimed Cai. "It's like a *Sleeping Beauty* garden."

Hannah laughed. "The previous owners weren't into gardening. Clearing this lot is one of the jobs Kathleen has lined up for us."

Carefully they manoeuvred the sign through the gate.

"See that?" said Hannah as they passed a wooden shed-like structure with a pointed roof and outside verandah. "That's going to be the Ocean Watch building. It's only temporary. Kathleen wants to build something bigger, but she has to get planning permission from the council first."

"The shed will be fine to get started in," Antonia said approvingly. "And the garden is a fantastic size. Does Kathleen have a boat?"

"Yes," Hannah nodded. "The sailing club is letting her keep it there until she gets the garden straight, even though it's a motorboat."

Nearing the house, Antonia felt a flutter of nerves. What would Kathleen be like? Would she mind them arriving so early on a Sunday morning? And would she see the funny side of them bringing her an

abandoned sign when she had enough junk of her own to sort out?

Antonia felt a sudden wave of homesickness for Claudia and Sea Watch.

Chapter Five

"I can't wait to see Kathleen's face when she sees this coffee sign!"

There was a twinkle in Hannah's eyes as she knocked on the back door.

"She won't mind us coming here so early, will she?" asked Antonia anxiously.

"Who, Kathleen?" Hannah laughed. "Of course not! She's always up early."

From the other side of the door came the sound of a bolt scraping open and a key turning in a lock. The door swung wide and a petite woman with short grey hair stood beaming at them. Kathleen was dressed in a stylish jumper and skinny jeans. She looked very glamorous and wore pale pink lipstick and mascara.

Antonia couldn't stop staring. She'd imagined Kathleen to look more like Claudia who was tall with wild, curly hair and usually wore old clothes.

"Antonia, Cai, this is Kathleen Abbot. Kathleen, meet Antonia Lee and Cai Pacific," Hannah announced in a formal tone before adding in her normal voice, "Look, Kathleen, we brought you a moving-in present. We pulled it out of the sea."

Kathleen glanced at the rusty coffee sign and roared with laughter.

"Thank you very much. Most of my friends gave me chocolates and pot plants when I moved here. This is much more exciting. I'll put it in the garden to remind me of you all."

"You're going to keep it?" Antonia was astonished.

"Of course! This is your first 'rescue' for Ocean Watch. Come on in. Breakfast is almost ready. You can tell me all about it over fried egg, bacon and sausages."

"Sounds lovely," said Cai, hurriedly pulling off his shoes.

For a moment Antonia was surprised that Kathleen had been expecting them. Then, noticing the silver dolphin hanging round her

neck, she realised that Kathleen would have known about Vision's call too.

A delicious smell was drifting from an enormous frying pan. Antonia's stomach growled hungrily as she followed everyone through the utility room and into the kitchen.

"Sit down," said Kathleen, pointing to a pine table with six chairs. "Hannah, you can get the knives and forks out for me. Is tea all right for everyone or are you coffee drinkers?"

"Tea, please." Antonia and Cai shared a smile as they sat at the table.

Over a huge breakfast, Antonia, Cai and Hannah told Kathleen about their rescue mission.

"Thank goodness you managed to help the seal by yourselves. I'm going to have to get

my skates on to make room for more animals here," said Kathleen with a slight frown.

"*More* animals?" questioned Hannah. "I thought you weren't taking any in at the moment, seeing as you've only just moved."

Kathleen turned slightly pink. "Well, you know how it is," she said vaguely. "People know I take in injured creatures so I can hardly turn them away when they arrive with a distressed animal, can I?"

"What is it this time?" Hannah sounded stern, but her mouth twitched in amusement.

"A seagull with a broken wing and a hedgehog that looks like it was clipped by a car," said Kathleen. "I've got them both in the lounge. Finish your breakfast then you can come and see."

When they'd had enough to eat, Antonia and Hannah cleared the table while Cai stacked the dishwasher. Kathleen's lounge was at the back of the house with double doors leading on to a patio. All of her furniture was pushed to one end of the room and at the other end were two cages. The first held a sad-looking gull whose right wing was taped to his side.

Even though Antonia knew Kathleen was experienced in dealing with sick animals she couldn't help but run a professional eye over the bird. Kathleen had done a good job, neatly securing the tape in front of the bird's feet to allow him to move around, and she had only given him a shallow dish of water so he couldn't drown if he toppled into it.

"I've had the bird for a couple of days now and he's much more stable. When I first taped his wing up, he kept falling over," said Kathleen, smiling directly at Antonia.

Antonia turned pink. She was used to Claudia reading her mind, but hadn't considered that Kathleen might be able to as well. Or was her comment just a coincidence? Antonia concentrated for a moment, listening for Kathleen's voice inside her head, but Kathleen was speaking out loud again.

"The hedgehog came in last night. She's not too badly hurt. I'll probably let her go in a day or two. She was full of fleas though. Luckily I managed to find the flea treatment among the unpacked boxes."

"She's really sweet," said Cai as the hedgehog

pushed her nose against the bars, making funny snuffling noises at his outstretched finger. "Will you set her free in your garden?"

"Yes," said Kathleen. "It's a hedgehog's paradise out there. Would you like a look round?"

"Yes, please," Cai and Antonia said together.

Cai's description of a *Sleeping Beauty* garden was a good one. Antonia had never seen such a wild place before. The shed was bigger than she'd first realised because the back was almost engulfed by a blackberry bush.

"There's a few late blackberries if anyone fancies them." Kathleen pointed to a cluster of plump black fruit.

"Cai?" asked Hannah.

Cai groaned. "Not me. After such an

enormous breakfast I couldn't eat another thing. I could do with some exercise to work it off. Can we start helping you, Kathleen?"

"That would be brilliant. The shed needs clearing first. Then I can move the animals out of my lounge. You can stay to lunch if you like. You'd better ring your mum and check that's all right with her, Hannah."

"Mum will be cool. I'll tell her not to expect us for lunch in case she gets something in," said Hannah.

She went inside to use the phone while Kathleen unlocked the shed. The door opened to reveal a mountain of junk.

"Wow!" said Cai. "How did you manage to pack all that inside?"

"I didn't," said Kathleen. "That lot belongs

to the people who lived here before me. They didn't bother to take it with them."

"That's a racing bike," said Antonia, pointing. "They're expensive."

"More money than sense, some people," Kathleen sniffed. "Anything good we'll sell on eBay and use the money to help set up Ocean Watch."

"We'll make three piles then," said Antonia. "EBay, recycle and dump. Hopefully we can sell or recycle most of the stuff. It's better than throwing it away."

"I've got a pack of disposable gloves up at the house," said Kathleen. "You'll need rubbish bags too. I'll just go and get everything." She hurried off, leaving Antonia and Cai alone.

Antonia stood still for a moment, trying to

shake off the sense of unease that had suddenly come over her. They had to get Ocean Watch up and running as soon as possible. She stepped forward and pulled a broken spade out of the shed.

"I'm starting the recycling pile here. This can easily be mended."

"This is going to take ages," said Cai.

"I know," said Antonia desperately. "We're only here until Wednesday. I hope that gives us enough time."

Cai picked up a punctured football and added it to the recycling pile.

"We'll do what we can," he said.

Chapter Six

They worked hard, stopping only for a quick lunch of homemade soup and hot crusty rolls with cheese and ham. As the shed got emptier, Antonia, Cai and Hannah grew dirtier and dirtier.

"At last! I can see the back wall," cried

Antonia as she lifted up a cardboard box full of old flowerpots.

"Hooray!" cheered Cai.

"So there is a back. I was beginning to think the shed was never-ending," said Hannah.

Kathleen looked outside at the blackening sky. "I hate these winter evenings. It gets dark too early. We'll have to stop soon. There's probably just enough time to finish clearing the shed. Then we'll put everything we're keeping or eBaying back in the garage as it looks like it might rain. The rubbish can stay out in the garden. I'll take it to the dump tomorrow with the recycling. I'm glad to see there's not that much to throw away."

"It looks like it's getting windy too." Antonia pushed her long blonde hair out of her face as she put a deckchair on the keep pile.

When the shed was finally empty, it was much bigger than everyone had realised. They gathered inside, discussing how best to use the space.

Hannah wrinkled her nose. "It smells."

"Tomorrow we'll clean it out and paint the walls. I've got a huge can of whitewash in the garage. That will get rid of the smell," said Kathleen. "And we'll put your coffee sign out on the verandah!"

"I can't wait to get Ocean Watch up and running," said Hannah impatiently. "It's going to be great. Are you going to take on volunteers like Claudia does?"

"One thing at a time," said Kathleen, laughing. "There's the garden to clear first. But yes, I'll definitely need to recruit some volunteers."

When they'd finished bundling the things that Kathleen thought would be useful or saleable into the garage, it was almost dark.

"I'll run you home in the car," she said as everyone filed back up to the house.

"What are you going to do about water?" asked Antonia as she waited for her turn to wash her hands in the utility room sink.

"For the shed? We're going to have to bring it down from the house in buckets. Unless..." Kathleen paused thoughtfully before continuing, "...maybe I should use the utility room as a temporary treatment room for now and keep the shed for

rehabilitation and general things. Obviously the new Ocean Watch building will have tap water, but it's going to be a while before I get planning permission, and then it has to be built."

"That's a brilliant idea," said Hannah enthusiastically. "We definitely need a treatment room with water."

"Yes," Antonia agreed. "You never know when there's going to be an emergency." She felt a rush of anxiety. They'd made a good start on the temporary Ocean Watch building, but suddenly it didn't seem enough. Vowing to work even harder the following day, she scrubbed her hands clean.

Kathleen gave everyone a small bar of chocolate to eat on the way home. "Something

to keep you going that won't spoil your tea," she said as she handed them out.

There were spots of rain on Kathleen's car when Antonia climbed in, munching her chocolate. She struggled to get the door shut against the wind.

"What a horrible evening," Kathleen shivered. She started the engine and switched on the heater.

It was a short drive to Hannah's apartment and the car was only just beginning to get warm when they arrived. Antonia climbed out and ran straight inside. It was raining heavily and in the few paces it took to get there she was soaked.

"Phew!" said Hannah. "I hope we're not going out for tea tonight. It's so wet."

They clattered into Hannah's apartment and hung their coats up to dry. Mrs Davies was pleased to see them.

"Are you hungry?" she asked. "I thought we'd ring for pizza."

They spent a fun evening eating tea while watching a film. Antonia particularly enjoyed herself as her mum never let her eat in front of the television. The film was so funny that Antonia finally managed to rid herself of the sense of unease that had been bothering her since yesterday. In the softly lit flat with the curtains drawn against the dark, wet night everything felt safe and under control. There was nothing to worry about. Ocean Watch would soon be up and running.

Later, as she lay in bed, listening to the wind and rain rattling on the window, Antonia touched her silver dolphin charm. Its soft body quivered against her fingers. Reassured, Antonia fell asleep.

The following morning Antonia, Cai and Hannah got up and had an early breakfast. They were piling their dirty dishes into the dishwasher when Mrs Davies wandered in, still wearing her dressing gown.

"Once I'm ready, I'll run you to Kathleen's in the car," she offered.

Antonia held her breath, hoping Hannah would refuse the offer. There wasn't time to wait for Mrs Davies. Antonia wanted to get going now. To her relief, Hannah shook her

head. "Thanks, Mum, but it's not far. We'll be there before you have time to dress."

Mrs Davies looked disappointed. "Oh, all right then. Anyone want a cup of tea before you all disappear?"

"No, thanks, but you're welcome to come to Kathleen's with us," said Hannah mischievously. "We could do with the extra hands."

Mrs Davies laughed. "No, thank you! I'd better get on with some of my own work. I've plenty to do."

The sky was grey, but at least it was dry and the wind had dropped. Antonia turned up the collar of her coat and buried her cold nose in it. They hurried to Kathleen's then stood on her doorstep ringing the bell for ages.

"Maybe she's in the garden," said Cai. "She might be loading her car with stuff for the dump."

They were about to go round the back and look when a dishevelled-looking Kathleen, wearing an enormous pair of gloves, appeared.

"Nice gloves," said Hannah, giggling.

"Squirrel trouble," answered Kathleen, by way of explanation.

"You've got a squirrel?" asked Hannah. "When did that come in?"

"Last night. He's got an injured paw. You wouldn't think so though. When I opened the cage to feed him this morning, he escaped and I'm still trying to catch him."

Kathleen opened the lounge door by a crack then shut it quickly when everyone had squeezed inside.

"There he is, on the curtain. Oh! He's so sweet!" exclaimed Antonia.

The squirrel was hanging from the curtain with his tail looped over his back like a furry question mark. There was a neat white bandage wrapped round his front left paw. He eyed Antonia suspiciously as she stepped towards him.

"It's OK, boy. I'm not going to hurt you." Antonia continued talking to the squirrel until she was close enough to reach up and lift him down.

"Careful!" warned Kathleen. "Don't touch him. Squirrels can have a nasty bite."

But there was no chance of Antonia getting close enough to touch the squirrel. With a defiant flick of his tail, he ran higher up the

curtains then, with an amazing leap, landed on the settee.

"A gymnast squirrel," commented Cai.

"Help me catch him," said Kathleen, advancing on the squirrel with open arms. "But don't touch him. Not under any circumstance!"

The squirrel waited for Kathleen to get within a whisker's length of him before scurrying across the top of the settee and jumping on to an armchair.

Cai grabbed the squirrel's empty cage and advanced towards him, forcing him into a corner. With an agitated chirrup, the squirrel darted round Cai and ran back up the curtains. He went right to the top and, whiskers twitching, sat watching everyone with a smug expression.

Kathleen was getting irritated. "We'll need a stepladder to reach him now. I wonder where it is..."

"In the utility room cupboard," Hannah reminded her. "I'll get it."

The squirrel was very cheeky. Chuckling at his antics, Antonia watched him swinging from the curtain.

Kathleen positioned the stepladder by the curtains and Cai stood at the bottom with the squirrel's cage. Slowly she began climbing up the rungs, mumbling softly to the squirrel as she went. Whiskers quivering, grey body hunched, the squirrel watched her. Each time she moved up a step, Kathleen stopped, hoping to reassure the squirrel that she meant no harm. Reaching the last rung, she slowly

stretched out her arms. Antonia held her breath.

She'd done it. Clever Kathleen had caught the squirrel! But as she wrapped her hands round his body, the squirrel wriggled free and raced down the curtain. Startled, Kathleen wobbled and only managed to save herself by grabbing a handful of curtain.

"Typical!" she exclaimed.

Chapter Seven

Hannah couldn't stop laughing. Cai went after the squirrel, trapping him in a corner of the room.

"Help me," he called.

Antonia ran to his side and together they managed to herd the squirrel inside his cage.

"Got you!" said Cai triumphantly, closing the door. The squirrel chattered angrily,

but Cai ignored him and carried the cage back to the other end of the lounge, setting it down near the hedgehog.

"Well done," said Kathleen. "I hope that paw heals soon and I can let him go. He's trouble, that one."

Idly Antonia wondered if her healing magic would work on the squirrel's paw. Should she ask Kathleen if she could give it a go? She didn't want to seem like she was showing off, but it would be a great help if the squirrel was fit enough to be released back into the wild. Antonia took a deep breath, steeling herself to say something, when she suddenly realised that her magic wouldn't work. How could it when the dolphins hadn't called for her help!

"Antonia, I asked if you were ready." Hannah gave her a quizzical look.

"Oh! Sorry. Yes, of course." Antonia didn't have a clue what she was supposed to be ready for, but she followed Hannah to the utility room.

"Washing the shed," hissed Cai in her ear. He gave her a knowing smile and muttered, "Miles away again."

Antonia grinned back. Although Cai couldn't actually read her mind, he knew her so well that sometimes it felt like he could!

"Let's get started then," she said cheerfully.

Hannah rifled through the utility room cupboards and found plastic aprons and disposable gloves. The aprons were too big so they wound the straps round their backs and tied them at their tummies.

"These will keep us nice and dry," said Antonia as she filled two buckets with warm water and soap.

"There are only two mops," said Hannah, backing out of a cupboard.

"How about you two have the mops and I go to the dump with Kathleen?" suggested Cai.

"Brilliant idea! There's not that much rubbish, but there's lots to go for recycling. I could do with an extra pair of hands," said Kathleen approvingly.

Antonia and Hannah each took a mop and a bucket of water and Cai carried a broom to the shed for them. He left them sweeping out the dirt before they washed the floor. It was very dusty and when the sweeping was done,

Antonia and Hannah stood outside to let the air clear.

"Eew!" coughed Antonia. "Gross!"

She gulped at the fresh air until she began to feel lightheaded. Then suddenly she realised another sensation was sweeping over her. *Vision!* He was about to call.

"Ready to start mopping?" asked Hannah.

Antonia had been about to nod, but no sooner had Hannah dunked her mop into the soapy water than Antonia felt her silver dolphin charm flutter against her neck. Hannah stopped work and leant the mop against the wall.

Silver Dolphin, we need you. Vision's voice rang out in Antonia's head.

I hear your call, she answered silently. A shrill whistle filled the shed.

"Vision, I hear your call," said Hannah, racing out of the door. She pulled the gate open and they squeezed through it together.

The estuary path was muddy after the rain. Feet squelching and sliding, Antonia ran as fast as she could to answer Vision's call. Poor Cai! Antonia knew he'd be upset to have missed this. Being a Silver Dolphin was a responsibility they both took very seriously.

It was easier going on the sand dunes as they were damp and the sand held together instead of sliding underfoot. Antonia and Hannah scrambled up them and down the other side. The tide was in and so the beach was much smaller today. Antonia pulled off her disposable gloves then her shoes, socks and apron. Hannah did the same and they left their

things in a pile. Wet sand splattered up their legs as they ran towards the grey waves.

Gritting her teeth against the cold, Antonia bravely waded into the sea. As the water came up to her thighs, she dived in and began swimming. Immediately her legs fused together and kicked like a dolphin's tail. Antonia forgot the cold and, using her hands like fins, propelled herself along. She loved the way her body arched in and out of the sea like a real dolphin. Whistling for joy, Antonia swam faster.

"We're going in the same direction as last time," clicked Hannah, panting a little as she caught Antonia up.

Antonia had noticed that too. She wondered why Vision had called them. Antonia and

Hannah swam on. After a while they could feel vibrations. Looking up, Antonia saw three dolphins, their silver heads bobbing in the sea. Hannah pulled ahead and stopped in front of the largest.

"Silver Dolphins, thank you for answering my call," clicked Vision, rubbing her on the nose.

Antonia hung back while Hannah rubbed noses with Vision, Lulu and Rolly. Then she greeted the dolphins.

"Dad said we could play when you're done," squeaked Lulu.

Vision clicked a laugh. "I did say that, but first the Silver Dolphins have a job to complete and it may take a while. There's some rubbish that needs clearing away."

Vision swam towards the shore, stopping as the water grew shallower. "I can't go any closer, but you can see from here."

Antonia followed Vision's line of sight and her mouth dropped open in amazement. Wherever had that come from?

Chapter Eight

"Is that a table?" Antonia couldn't help being surprised even though she was used to finding all sorts of strange items littering the seas.

"Looks so," said Hannah as they waded towards the object. "It's the sort pubs and cafés put outside."

The table lay on its back. Surf frothed round its skyward-pointing legs. One leg was merely a jagged stump. Hannah examined the table carefully.

"I'm almost certain this came from the café garden too," she said. "They've got ones exactly like this."

"But how did it get down here?" asked Antonia. "Is someone pushing things off the cliff?"

"I don't know," said Hannah thoughtfully. "It didn't look like anyone had been near the place, did it?"

"Apart from when the trees were cut down," said Antonia. "It was really windy last night. Maybe it got blown over the edge."

"Yes! That's it!" Hannah exclaimed. "It got blown over. Luckily it landed here and not a bit further round where the seals are."

On second glance, Antonia thought that the table looked far too sturdy to have been blown from the cliff top, but she didn't say anything. "What are we going to do with it?" she asked.

"Let's get it out of the sea and put it on the beach while we decide," Hannah suggested.

Positioning themselves at opposite ends of the table, they lifted it up and carried it on to the sand.

"A bit more," puffed Hannah. "Here, that should do. It's far enough back not to get washed out by the tide."

"We can't leave it here!" exclaimed Antonia.

"No, of course not," agreed Hannah. "But it's not the sort of thing you can throw in the nearest bin and it's too heavy for us to carry back to Kathleen's. I thought if we left it on the beach, she could come and collect it in the car."

"That's a good idea," said Antonia. "We'd better find out where we are. There's a footpath over there. Let's see where it goes."

The footpath led between a gap in the cliffs and after several twists and turns opened up into a field.

"It's a car park." Antonia pointed to a small wooden hut with a man inside reading a newspaper. There was only one car in the field and it looked like it belonged to the car-park attendant.

"I wonder if he wants a table," said Hannah. "He could sit outside on nice days."

"It's only got three legs," Antonia reminded her.

"Good point." Hannah sighed. "That's a shame. We'll have to get Kathleen to come and pick it up – as if she hasn't got enough to do."

"At this rate Kathleen will be able to set up a café in her own garden soon. Maybe she should hire a lorry and clear the old café's garden if she's going to end up with all their furniture," said Antonia, half teasing, but with a note of seriousness.

"Very funny," Hannah laughed. "Let's go back now. Lulu and Rolly are waiting to play."

Surreptitiously Antonia glanced at her watch.

She really wanted to play with the dolphins, but it was already mid-morning and they had lots to do.

"A quick game," Hannah added.

It would be fun to play with Lulu and Rolly and a quick game should be all right. With any luck, Kathleen and Cai would be back by now. They might even have mopped the floor. Antonia felt guilty about playing with the dolphins when Cai was busy, even though she knew he wouldn't mind.

"Race you back to the beach," she shouted, sprinting away.

"Cheat," called Hannah, galloping after her. "You had a head start."

Antonia reached the beach first and wedged some rocks against the table's three

legs to make doubly sure that it wasn't going anywhere. Hannah arrived hot on her heels.

"I nearly beat you," she said with a grin.

Antonia found a piece of crinkly brown seaweed draped on a rock like a lost scarf. She snatched it up. "This is perfect for seaweed tag. I'll be it."

They ran back into the water, gasping at its coldness until their legs melded together and they didn't notice any more. Lulu and Rolly were waiting for them a short way out to sea.

"Seaweed tag, three waves' head start," clicked Antonia, waving the seaweed in the air.

Everyone shot in different directions, leaving Antonia bobbing in the water on her own. Well, almost on her own... Away to her left a grey head nodded in the water.

Antonia cried out in delight. "A seal!"

For a moment she was distracted as she watched the seal swim closer to the shore. Then, veering away, he swam round the headland. Antonia sighed contentedly then whistled, "Three waves, ready or not – I'm coming!"

They played five games of seaweed tag. Lulu and Rolly were bigger cheats than Bubbles, Antonia's dolphin friend, but it was great fun trying to get the better of them. When everyone had had a turn at being it, Antonia called a halt to the game. "We have to get back," she said.

"Spoilsport," said Lulu, splashing her with water.

"Spoilsport yourself," retorted Antonia, good-naturedly splashing Lulu back.

"Water fight!" clicked Rolly, joyfully smacking his tail on the sea's surface.

It was impossible not to join in. Antonia splashed as hard as she could, spraying anyone who came near with salty water.

"We really have to go," said Hannah at last when everyone stopped for a rest.

Antonia nodded. Cai would be waiting to hear about their rescue. She couldn't wait to tell him about the table. Imagine his surprise!

Lulu and Rolly swam with the Silver Dolphins back to the beach where they'd left their things.

"Come again soon," clicked Lulu, rubbing noses goodbye.

"We will," Hannah answered.

Antonia said nothing as an unpleasant feeling washed over her. *Get a grip!* she told

herself. But even as the feeling subsided, Antonia was left with a sense of unease.

She knew she would be seeing the dolphins very soon, and next time it wouldn't be to play.

Chapter Nine

Cai and Kathleen had been busy in their absence. They'd mopped the shed floor twice and were just finishing loading the car with another pile of rubbish and recycling for the dump.

"The shed walls need scrubbing with water and then it's ready to paint," said Cai.

"We'll do that while you go to the tip," Hannah offered.

"Thanks. I'll stop off and collect that table you found too. I'd better take a saw or I might not get it in the car. You stay here this time, Cai. We're going to be tight for space."

Kathleen went to the garage and came back carrying a large saw. She put it in the boot and slammed it shut.

"Who's that coming up the drive?" asked Cai.

A young woman carrying a baby on her hip was striding purposefully towards them.

Kathleen smiled at her and called out, "Hello."

"Hello," said the woman in a clipped tone. "I'm Jane Row, your neighbour."

"Kathleen Abbot." Kathleen held out her hand. "Nice to meet you, Jane. I've been meaning to pop round and introduce myself, but I've been so busy moving in." She held out her hand for a few seconds longer then dropped it when it became obvious that Jane wasn't going to shake it.

"The thing is," said Jane defensively, "I've seen wild animals being brought in here. People are saying that you're running a rescue centre for them. Is that right?"

"Almost," said Kathleen enthusiastically. "I'm in the middle of setting up a marine conservation charity called Ocean Watch. These are my helpers, Hannah, Cai and Antonia."

"Is this going to be in the house?"

"Mainly in the garden shed," said Kathleen. She waved at the car. "We've just been having a clear-out."

"Well, I want you to stop." Jane stared defiantly at Kathleen.

Antonia almost gasped out loud. How rude! Why did Jane want Kathleen to stop? Didn't she realise how important their work was?

"We've been living here for three years. It's a peaceful road and most of the residents have families. We don't want a business stuck in the middle of us."

"It's not a business. I'm setting up a charity," said Kathleen patiently.

"A charity that takes in dangerous wild animals," said Jane. "If that isn't bad enough, we'll probably get rats next."

"Rats!"

"Wild animals and rubbish encourage rats," said Jane firmly.

"Which is precisely why I'm taking this rubbish to the dump," said Kathleen icily. "Well-looked-after animals do not attract rats."

Jane snorted. "They might! You'll be storing animal feed and straw, both of which attract rats. Then there's the noise you'll be making and all the comings and goings of your visitors. I expect you'll be opening to the public like some kind of zoo."

Antonia couldn't help herself. She didn't mean to be rude, but it was clear that Jane didn't have a clue what she was talking about.

"Our friend Claudia runs a marine charity called Sea Watch from her garden," she said

earnestly. "It doesn't bother anyone. There's no mess, no noise and definitely no rats."

Jane glared at her. "This is my home. I do not intend to live next door to a business or charity or whatever you want to call it and I will not tolerate rats. There's the baby to think of."

At this moment the baby's face crumpled at her angry voice and he started crying.

"There, there," said Jane, shooting Antonia a look that clearly blamed her for upsetting the baby.

Kathleen inhaled sharply. "You are very much mistaken. Once Ocean Watch is up and running, you will see how wrong you are. Now, if you'll excuse me, there's work to do."

"Don't think that's the end of it." Jane raised

her voice. "You can't run your business from here."

"It's *not* a business. It's a *charity*," repeated Kathleen.

"If you won't stop then I'll get the council out. I bet you don't have planning permission."

Kathleen went rigid and Antonia could see she was very angry.

"Go ahead then!" Kathleen almost shouted at Jane. "Like I said, we're busy."

"Don't worry, I'm on my way. I wouldn't stay a second longer in this rat-infested place if you paid me," Jane shouted disdainfully. "There're laws to deal with people like you. Setting up illegal businesses and exploiting children. I'm ringing the council. They'll shut you down in no time."

Jane marched up the drive, her hips waddling and the baby bouncing with each angry step.

Kathleen leant against the car. She was trembling. Hannah put her arms round her. "Nasty woman," she soothed. "Forget her. She's not worth it."

"But what if she's right? What if I do need planning permission to set up Ocean Watch and the council refuse to give it to me? Did Claudia have permission? I didn't think to ask when we spoke on the phone last week."

Antonia and Cai shrugged helplessly. Claudia had set up Sea Watch before either of them had joined.

"Ring the council and ask," suggested Antonia. "You were going to apply for planning

permission for the new building anyway. So ring them now."

"Yes." Kathleen was dazed. "That's what I'll do." She checked her watch. "The dump closes at lunchtime. I'd better go and get rid of this stuff first. I'll ring when I get back."

"Will you be all right on your own? Are you sure you don't want one of us to come with you?"

"I'll be fine, thanks." Smiling bravely, Kathleen drew herself up. "We'll carry on as we were. You wash the shed while I'm gone."

She drove slowly away, waving her hand out of the window until she reached the end of the road. Hannah turned to Antonia and Cai, her shoulders drooping dejectedly. "Is there any point in scrubbing the shed walls

before Kathleen's spoken to the council? I mean, what if they say no to us having Ocean Watch here?"

"Of course they won't say no! Claudia's allowed to run Sea Watch from her home, isn't she?"

Antonia sounded much more confident than she felt. A new thought was playing on her mind. What if someone complained about Sea Watch? Would Claudia be made to close her charity too? A cold chill settled in Antonia's stomach. She wouldn't think about it. There was no point worrying until Kathleen had found out the facts.

"Come on," she said briskly. "There's work to do."

Chapter Ten

It was hot, dirty work scrubbing out the shed. Antonia's hair felt itchy with dust and Cai and Hannah had grimy smudges on their faces. They had started at the bottom of the first wall, which quickly proved to be a big mistake. Once they'd finished the bottom half, Cai volunteered to scrub the top. But as he set to work, using Kathleen's stepladder to

reach, the dirt trickled down and messed up the bit they'd already cleaned.

"No!" squealed Hannah in disgust. "We didn't think of that. We'll have to start again."

"Lucky we only did one wall," said Cai.

Antonia worked harder than anyone, scrubbing at the walls like a demon. It was the only way to forget her anxieties about Ocean Watch and Sea Watch. The shed smelt much better for a good clean, but everyone agreed it still needed painting.

"The window's not very big and it's quite dark in here. Whitewash will brighten it up," said Cai.

"Kathleen's going to get electricity put in too so we can have lights," said Hannah.

They carried the buckets, mops, brushes and

stepladder back to the house and were putting everything away when Kathleen arrived back. After saying a quick hello, she went straight to the kitchen and took the telephone directory from the dresser.

"West Wood Council," she muttered as she flicked through the pages. "S, T, U, V, W… here it is." Squinting at the page, she jotted the number down on a scrap of paper.

Antonia, Cai and Hannah sat in silence at the kitchen table as Kathleen punched the numbers on the telephone keypad. The phone rang three times before Kathleen was connected to the switchboard. Antonia flinched, scrunching her hands into tight balls. This was it!

"Planning control, please," said Kathleen.

Seconds later she was through, but as she

went to speak, she rolled her eyes and mouthed, "Voice mail."

Antonia nearly yelled with frustration. It seemed like everything was working against them. How much longer would they have to wait before they knew if Ocean Watch was allowed to operate?

Kathleen left a short message asking someone to call her back then hung up.

"According to that, everyone is out on site visits," she said. "They'll be back in the office tomorrow."

"Tomorrow's Cai and Antonia's last day," wailed Hannah. "They go home on Wednesday."

Kathleen spread out her hands in a gesture of helplessness. "There's nothing more I can do."

"I think we should carry on as we were going to," said Antonia. "It's not like we're deliberately breaking any laws. It's such a waste of time to stop now when what we're doing is probably fine."

She sounded much more confident than she felt and it did the trick.

"Antonia's right. We carry on as normal," said Kathleen. "It's almost lunchtime, so how about I make some cheese toasties and after that we'll paint the shed?"

Cai licked his lips. "Sounds like an excellent idea," he said.

They all helped get lunch. Kathleen buttered and toasted bread while Antonia sliced cheese, Hannah washed tomatoes and Cai emptied a huge packet of crisps into a bowl

for sharing. While the sandwiches were sizzling under the grill, Kathleen made steaming mugs of tea. It was a simple meal, but it felt like a feast. Antonia hadn't realised how hungry she was.

"These are excellent," said Cai appreciatively.

"I'm going to make them at home," said Hannah. "They're so easy I bet even Mum could do it."

"We should get our mums together sometime," said Cai. "Mine's hopeless at cooking too."

"You think that's a good idea?" Hannah raised an eyebrow.

As Antonia listened to her friends' banter, she realised they weren't going to have time to sit there much longer. A familiar sensation was coming over her. Any minute now Vision would call.

Antonia sat up in surprise. Two calls in one day! What did Vision need them for this time?

The doorbell rang, making everyone jump. Kathleen turned a shade paler.

"That better not be Jane," she said through gritted teeth.

"Do you want me to answer it?" asked Hannah.

"Thanks, but I'll go." Pushing back her chair, Kathleen stood up.

Antonia watched her through the partially open kitchen door. Suddenly her silver dolphin charm twitched. Antonia craned forward and was relieved to see it wasn't Jane at the door,

but a smartly dressed woman carrying a clipboard. A sales rep!

Her fingers curled protectively round her dolphin charm as it started vibrating.

Silver Dolphin, we need you.

There was urgency in Vision's voice and something else that Antonia didn't understand.

I hear your call, she answered, rising to her feet at the same time as Hannah and Cai.

Antonia glanced at Kathleen, hoping that she had heard the call too and wouldn't think they'd abandoned her to the sales rep. But as she ran out of the back door, the woman's voice rang out loud and clear. "Susan Birch, West Wood Council. We've had a complaint from one of your neighbours."

Antonia's heart thudded in her chest. No prizes for guessing where that had come from.

Silver Dolphins, come quickly.

You're hurt. Antonia suddenly realised why Vision sounded strange. He was in pain. *I'm on my way.*

Guiltily abandoning Kathleen to the lady from the council, Antonia ran down the garden. Cai and Hannah followed. It wasn't right leaving Kathleen to deal with Susan Birch all by herself, but what else could they do? Vision was hurt and needed help. Antonia dashed through the garden gate and nearly collided with a couple out walking their dog.

"Sorry," she called out, dashing past them.

The wind had picked up and it snatched at her clothes as she ran towards the beach.

Antonia leant forward, fighting against it, refusing to let the wind hold her back. Her silver dolphin charm thrashed against her neck in encouragement.

Vision, I'm coming, she promised.

Antonia, Hannah and Cai hurtled on to the beach like rockets. Climbing the sand dunes with long, powerful strides, they kicked off their shoes and socks when they reached the other side and ran towards the sea.

Chapter Eleven

ntonia barely noticed how cold the water was as she splashed into the sea. As soon as it was deep enough to swim, she dived into the waves, using her hands like flippers to propel her along. Almost at once her legs melded together as a tail and she swam like a dolphin. Antonia dived in and out of the

waves, her body flashing through the air in graceful arcs. She could hear Cai and Hannah behind her, but there was no time to wait for them.

A short way out to sea she spotted two dolphins, Vision and Dancer. Antonia was relieved. Vision couldn't be that badly hurt then, could he? But as she drew closer, she realised she'd been mistaken. Vision's handsome face was badly swollen. For a moment Antonia was so startled she almost stopped swimming. Quickly she pulled herself together. Vision needed help.

"What happened?" clicked Antonia as she closed the gap between them.

"I got hit on the head by falling wood." Vision looked affronted and confused.

Antonia swam closer and, when she was almost nose to nose with the dolphin leader, she began to examine him. A trickle of blood was running down his face and it didn't take long to find the wound, between his nose and blowhole.

The sea was extremely choppy. Antonia bobbed up and down, her legs kicking rhythmically as she concentrated on keeping close to Vision. She cupped her hands together and splashed the wound with sea water. Each time she washed the blood away, more oozed from the cut.

"Is it serious?" asked Dancer.

Antonia gave up on the cleaning and examined the cut. To her relief it was nowhere near as bad as she'd first thought.

"It's nasty, but it looks worse than it is," she said.

Gently she placed her hands directly on Vision's head, pushing the edges of the cut together.

Heal.

A warm sensation flooded down her arms and into her hands, making them prickle.

Heal.

Antonia kept her fingers firmly on the wound, pressing it together as she willed it to mend. From the corner of her eye she saw Cai and Hannah arrive. She heard them talking to Dancer in soft, anxious clicks. Then they fell silent. Glancing up, Antonia saw Hannah watching her in amazement. After a bit the warm feeling in Antonia's fingers lessened.

Carefully, hardly daring to look, she raised her hands. The wound had completely healed, leaving only a faint line to show where the cut had been.

"Thank you, Silver Dolphin," said Vision, nuzzling his nose in her hair.

"It was nothing." Antonia felt her face redden.

"It was everything." Dancer stroked her hair with a flipper.

"That was incredible," whispered Hannah. "I've never seen you heal a wound before."

"Thanks." Antonia knew how lucky she was to have such strong powers.

"Dancer said you were hit by this," said Cai. With Hannah's help he was holding on to a sturdy piece of wood with a jagged end.

"Yes," agreed Vision. "We were by the seal beach when it happened. There was a rumbling noise then this flew through the air and caught me on the head."

"We thought it would be quicker if we swam to meet you. Vision insisted we brought the wood along too," clicked Dancer.

"You know what this is?" asked Cai excitedly.

Antonia was tired from healing Vision and struggling to keep afloat in the choppy sea.

"What?" she asked blankly.

"It's a table leg," said Cai. "I bet it came from the table you and Hannah found this morning."

"You said you heard a rumbling noise?" Hannah questioned Vision.

"Yes," said Vision.

"I don't like it." Hannah looked thoughtful.

"The rumbling might have been a car engine," said Cai.

"Maybe," said Hannah. "But I think we should get Kathleen to drive us up to the café and take a look. Things falling off the cliff is becoming a habit. It can't be coincidence. Something's going on up there."

Antonia didn't like it either. Something wasn't right. They had to discover what the problem was and deal with it before there was a more serious accident. She opened her mouth to agree, but a gust of wind blew her hair into her mouth. Antonia spat it out.

"The wind is getting stronger," said Vision sympathetically. "There's a storm brewing. Thank you for your help, Silver Dolphins.

Better go home now before the sea gets too rough. Dancer, we must leave too. The pod will be waiting for us to take them out to sea."

"That's the best place to weather a storm," said Cai.

"It is," agreed Vision.

He swam forward, rubbing noses with each of the Silver Dolphins. Dancer rubbed noses with them too and stroked Antonia's hair with a flipper.

"Thank you, Silver Dolphin," she whispered.

"It was nothing," repeated Antonia, but inside she was glowing with happiness. The feeling lasted until Vision and Dancer were almost out of sight, their silver bodies flashing in and out of the iron-grey sea.

"We'd better get back and see if Kathleen's

all right," she said, guiltily remembering how they'd abandoned her to the council lady.

No one spoke on the way back to the beach. Furtively glancing at Cai and Hannah, Antonia could see they shared her anxieties about the future of Ocean Watch. They swam ashore, bracing themselves against the surf erupting in a seething mass of foam on the deserted beach. The sea water poured off them and soon their clothes were completely dry.

Antonia shivered, pulling the hood of her coat over her head to protect her from the wind. The moment she took her hands away, the hood blew down again. Cold as she was, Antonia laughed.

"Let's race back," said Hannah. "That'll warm us up."

Running into the wind was hard work, especially as they were carrying the table leg. Antonia's face felt stretched as the wind tugged at her skin and pulled at her eyes and mouth. But she was lovely and warm by the time she arrived back at Kathleen's and her damp hair had dried too. It took all three of them to open the gate and ease it shut without having it ripped from their hands by the wind.

"It's blowing a gale," said Cai, snatching his fingers away before the gate slammed shut on them.

"Look, Kathleen's started painting the shed!" Hannah shouted.

Antonia's heart soared. Surely that was good news? Kathleen wouldn't be painting if the council lady was going to shut them down.

They ran over, giggling at the sight of Kathleen who'd covered her hair with a huge scarf.

"You've got paint on your nose," said Hannah.

"I expect that's an improvement!" Kathleen answered.

Antonia was impatient to know Ocean Watch's fate. "Sorry we left you. What happened with that lady?" she cut in.

Kathleen finished the bit she was painting then carefully placed her roller in the paint tray.

"I don't know! Susan Birch is a newly qualified planning officer. She doesn't think I'm breaking any laws, but she wasn't sure. She's coming back with a more senior colleague."

"When?" Antonia almost stamped her foot in exasperation.

"Tomorrow morning. Don't worry about it – I'm not. Everything's going to be fine, even if we do have to apply for planning permission." Kathleen sounded calm, but Antonia noticed her hands were shaking.

"Of course," Antonia smiled back at Kathleen. Inside, her stomach was churning. The feeling of doom she'd had before was back and this time it was much stronger. Slowly and deliberately Antonia said under her breath, "It's going to be fine."

But no matter how many times she repeated it, she couldn't quite believe it.

Chapter Twelve

Kathleen was keen to hear about their latest rescue mission as she examined the stumpy piece of wood.

"It certainly looks like it came from a table," she agreed. "We definitely ought to take a look round the café and see what's going on

up there. How about we go tomorrow, after our visitors have been?"

Antonia was torn between visiting the café straight away and staying put to get on with the jobs that needed doing at Kathleen's. The wind was very strong. What if something else got blown over the cliff? But there was so little time left to get Ocean Watch up and running before she and Cai went home. Of course the café visit could wait until tomorrow.

While Kathleen finished painting the shed, Antonia, Cai and Hannah worked in the utility room, sorting out the things that needed to go in it.

"We'll divide the disposable gloves, aprons and paper towels in half so we've some for

in here and some for Ocean Watch," said Hannah.

Here *and* Ocean Watch? It took a moment for Antonia to realise that Hannah meant the shed, but once she'd worked it out she liked it. Actually calling the shed Ocean Watch made it sound permanent, like it was definitely happening.

Kathleen had ordered lots of supplies including scissors, tweezers and bandages. They stacked everything they needed next to the sink.

"There's a cupboard to put all this in," said Hannah. "It's in the garage. It came as a flat pack so it needs putting together. There isn't time now, but we can build it tomorrow. We won't be able to move any of the animals

to Ocean Watch yet because of the wet paint."

"It's our last whole day tomorrow," said Antonia glumly. She was looking forward to going home and getting back to Sea Watch, but at the same time wanted to stay longer to help Hannah and Kathleen.

"I'm going to miss you both," said Hannah. "I'll ask Daisy, my best friend at school, to come and help, but it won't be as good as having other Silver Dolphins around."

"We'll miss you too," said Antonia.

"You could always invite us to stay again," said Cai cheekily. "And you can visit us any time."

"Yes! That'd be great," Antonia agreed enthusiastically. When Hannah had first

helped out at Sea Watch, Antonia hadn't been very friendly towards her. Now she was one of Antonia's closest friends. Next time Hannah visited, Antonia was determined to make sure she had a good time.

"It's a deal," said Hannah.

It was getting dark when all the jobs were finally done so Kathleen ran them home in the car.

"Watch your fingers in the car doors," she said. "It's even windier than yesterday."

"At least it's dry," said Hannah, but she spoke too soon. Almost at once it started to rain. By the time they arrived home, the rain was so heavy it was coming down in sheets. Hannah stood in the entrance hall, shaking her long red hair like a wet dog.

"Stop it! I'm getting wet," chuckled Cai.

They climbed the stairs to the first floor and were met by a delicious smell drifting along the corridor.

"That can't be coming from our flat!" Hannah was incredulous.

But it was! Mrs Davies opened the door wearing a brand-new red and white apron and brandishing a wooden spoon.

"Good, you're back," she said, ushering everyone inside. "Dinner's nearly ready."

"You've cooked!" Hannah was so surprised she went straight to the kitchen to see for herself.

"It wasn't that difficult," said Mrs Davies defensively. "Anyone would think I'm useless."

Wrapping her arms round her mum, Hannah gave her a big hug.

"You're a brilliant photographer," she said. "But you don't usually cook."

"I don't usually have any free time," said Mrs Davies, shooing her out of the kitchen. "Go and wash your hands."

Antonia thought she would have trouble sleeping that night. At first she lay in bed worrying about the visit from the planning department the following day. Outside it was blowing a gale. Rain splattered against the window and the wind shrieked and moaned. Antonia hoped Vision had led his dolphins safely out to sea.

Antonia's eyelids drooped and she fell asleep. Hours later she woke with a crick in her neck. The room was coal-black. Carefully,

so as not to wake Hannah, Antonia sat up and rubbed her neck. That felt better. She was about to snuggle down again when she felt a familiar sensation. Antonia tensed, knowing that Vision was about to call.

Silently she threw back the duvet and climbed down the bunk ladder. She groped around in the dark for her clothes. Her silver dolphin charm began to thrash against her neck and a shrill whistle rang out in the room. Antonia was startled. The charm usually started off by fluttering softly. This must be very serious! The noise woke Hannah who jumped out of bed and turned on the light.

Silver Dolphins, we need you.

Vision, I hear your call, Antonia answered

silently while Hannah spoke the same words out loud.

"Oh, my goodness!" Hannah exclaimed, glancing at her alarm. "It's five in the morning."

"It's urgent." Antonia tugged a jumper over her head.

"I know," said Hannah, touching her vibrating dolphin.

Cai beat them to the front door. He quietly unbolted it as the girls put on their shoes. In silence they tiptoed along the corridor, down the stairs and into the softly lit entrance hall. Hannah shivered.

"It's still raining, but it sounds like the wind's dropped."

They pulled up the hoods on their coats.

The rain was so heavy that soon they were soaked through.

"Lucky I brought this," said Cai, switching on a waterproof torch as they ran across the grass to the garden gate.

"I've got one too," said Antonia, switching on her torch.

The grass was slippery, forcing them to slow their pace. "Better to get there in one piece than not at all," muttered Hannah.

The path was even worse than the grass. Gingerly the Silver Dolphins ran along, feet squelching in the sticky mud. It was a relief to reach the sand dunes. The wet sand held firm as they climbed to the top and ran down the other side, torches swinging wildly. Leaving their shoes and torches at the bottom

of the dunes, they ran across the beach, wet sand splattering their clothes and oozing between their toes.

Hurry, Silver Dolphins. Vision's voice, loud and clear in Antonia's head, sounded desperate.

I'm coming, she silently answered.

Running even faster, Antonia hurtled across the beach with Cai and Hannah. At first the inky water sucked at their legs, holding them back. Antonia kept walking, concentrating on becoming a Silver Dolphin, then diving into the sea, she swam. Her legs melded together to kick like a tail and her hands paddled like flippers.

Antonia raced alongside Cai and Hannah, swimming even faster than real dolphins as they answered Vision's call for help.

Chapter Thirteen

ision's call was coming from the same direction as the cliff-top café. Deep down Antonia had expected it. Ignoring the cold rain splashing on her face, she swam on until she saw four shapes agitatedly swimming in the water.

Antonia reached the dolphins a body's length before Cai and Hannah.

There was no time for a friendly greeting. Even Lulu and Rolly looked serious. Antonia suddenly felt sick with anxiety.

"We came as fast as we could," panted Hannah, arriving with Cai.

"Silver Dolphins, thank goodness you're here. A terrible thing has happened," clicked Vision. "The storm caused a landslide on to the seals' beach. Lots of seals are injured and trapped. Please help them."

It was starting to get light. Antonia squinted at the beach and her insides turned ice-cold. Instead of golden sand there was a dirty mountain of soil, rocks and vegetation from the cliff top. At once Antonia swam towards the shore. Drawing closer she could hear the seals barking in distress. She glanced at Cai

and Hannah, swimming alongside her. "Hurry," she urged them.

The landslide was the worse disaster Antonia had ever seen. The mountain of fallen soil was huge. Injured and scared seals lay everywhere. As she waded through the surf, Antonia saw a massive tree lying across the beach. An outside table and a litter bin were tangled in its branches. Antonia rushed forward, tears stinging her eyes as she realised a seal was trapped under there too.

She scrambled towards him. Branches caught at her clothes and scratched her hands. Antonia hardly noticed. She fought her way forward until finally she reached the seal. He was a handsome male with a sleek grey coat.

"Steady, boy." Antonia spoke soothingly as

she pulled at the branch lying on top of him. Dried leaves fell from the branch, covering the seal in an orangey-brown blanket. The seal watched Antonia with soulful eyes.

"That's better. I can see you now." Antonia carefully brushed the leaves off the seal's coat to examine him. Miraculously, apart from a few scratches, he didn't seem to be injured.

"You've had a lucky escape," she told him. "Be patient. We'll soon have you out of there."

Cai and Hannah helped, snapping away the twigs and branches until finally the seal was able to wriggle clear.

"One down. But who do we help next?" Hannah stared at the beach in dismay. There were so many seals trapped by soil or fallen

branches that it was impossible to know where to start.

"Over there," said Cai, pointing to a seal whose tail was pinned by a rock. He ran over and began pushing the rock away.

"Oomph!" Cai grunted, his face reddening with exertion. "This one needs your help, Antonia."

Antonia went forward to give him a hand, her eyes widening at the livid red gash along the seal's tail.

"Steady there," she soothed as the seal, a female with huge eyes and freckled face, tried to pull away. The seal's whiskers twitched fearfully, her big brown eyes begging Antonia not to hurt her any more.

"I'm here to help."

Antonia sat down and ran her hand over the seal's soft coat until she reached the gash. Gently she placed her hands on either side of it and pushed.

Heal.

Antonia concentrated on helping the seal. A tingling sensation spread along her arms and into her hands. As the magic warmed her fingers, Antonia pressed the edges of the wound more firmly together.

Heal.

She was dimly aware of Hannah and Cai holding a fierce conversation.

Heal.

A final burst of warmth exploded in Antonia's fingers. She held them in place for a short while longer then slowly lifted them up. The wound

had closed, leaving a pale pink line in its place. The seal beat her tail in thanks.

"You're welcome," said Antonia, pushing her hair back from her face. "Now who's next?"

"We've been talking about that," said Cai. "There are too many for us to cope with on our own. We need help."

Claudia, thought Antonia automatically. But Claudia was too far away.

"We need Kathleen," said Hannah. "I don't suppose you've got a mobile phone, Antonia? If not, someone's going to have to go back for her."

Antonia shook her head. Even if she did own a mobile, she wouldn't have carried it into the sea!

Kathleen! Antonia willed her to hear her cry for help.

Kathleen, we need you.

Nothing.

Sadly Antonia realised that Kathleen couldn't hear her that way.

"I'll go back," said Cai decisively. "Antonia's the fastest swimmer, but we need her here to heal the injured seals."

"It's all right. I'll go," Hannah offered.

"Wait!" Antonia had an idea. She wasn't sure if it would work, but it was worth a try. She closed her eyes and thought about Claudia. Would she be awake yet?

Claudia?

A picture of her friend swam into her mind.

Claudia dressed in work clothes, pushing her unruly hair away from her sea-green eyes.

Claudia?

Antonia concentrated as hard as she could.

Silver Dolphin, is that you?

Yes! There's been an accident. A landslide at the seal beach. We need help. Can you tell Kathleen?

I'll ring her. Will she know where you are?

Tell her it's the beach beneath the café.

Antonia thought Kathleen would know where the seal beach was, but it was better to be sure.

Be strong, Silver Dolphin.

Antonia's head was suddenly silent. Antonia

was so relieved. Claudia had sensed this was serious. She'd gone to ring Kathleen straight away.

"Antonia?" Cai touched her arm.

She opened her eyes and smiled at Cai.

"Help's coming," she said.

"Is Kathleen… I mean, does she…"

"No, but Claudia's going to ring her," said Antonia.

Cai grinned back. "You're amazing," he said. "Both of you."

Antonia flushed. "We all are," she said warmly. "Come on. There's work to do."

They divided themselves up. Hannah and Cai freed trapped seals and Antonia healed them. It was hard, exhausting work. Antonia had never used her healing powers on so

many animals at the same time and she wasn't sure how long her magic would last. As they cleared up the debris, Hannah and Cai piled it into a corner of the beach to avoid further injuries. Their fingernails were black with dirt and their hands and faces were covered in scratches.

"We need an axe," said Hannah. "It'd be easier to clear this stuff if we could get rid of the fallen tree."

"It's enormous." Cai eyed the tree speculatively. Suddenly he leant forward. "Listen, did you hear that?"

Something in his tone made Antonia look up from the seal she had just finished healing. A plaintive cry like a kitten mewling came from under the tree.

Cai fell on the tree, tearing at the branches with his hands. Antonia and Hannah rushed over to join him.

"It's a seal," panted Cai. "I can just see it."

Chapter Fourteen

There was one branch in the way that was too thick to break with their bare hands. Antonia, Cai and Hannah pulled the smaller twigs and dead leaves from it until it was completely stripped. The naked branch lay over the seal, caging her in. The seal gave a weak bark of distress.

"Be strong," Antonia soothed her. "We're going to help you."

She looked around for something sharp. There was plenty to choose from. A flint-shaped stone caught her eye and she slipped down from the tree trunk to fetch it. The stone felt heavy in her hand, but would it be weighty enough for what she had in mind?

Holding it tightly, Antonia climbed back on to the fallen tree trunk, inching her way along it until she reached the branch. She leant forward, picking a spot where the branch was thinner. Antonia held the stone to the wood. With a sawing motion, she pushed it backwards and forwards.

Cut.

She concentrated on the stone, willing it to

slice through the wood. A tingling sensation passed down her arms and slowly moved along to her hands. It was sluggish and felt lukewarm. Antonia was tired and her magic was weakening. She stopped sawing. Closing her eyes, she took a long deep breath in. She held it for a couple of seconds then slowly let it out. She repeated this a few times before placing the stone back on the branch.

Cut.

Her fingers prickled. Antonia pressed harder, willing the magic into the stone. Something tickled her nostrils, making her want to sneeze. Damp sawdust! Antonia sawed harder, forcing the stone to cut further through the branch until she realised Cai was shaking her arm. His eyes were bright with emotion.

"Let us help," he urged. "We could probably snap it now."

Antonia pulled back and stretched her aching fingers. The warmth had gone, leaving them feeling as cold and limp as a jellyfish. Her eyes widened at the branch half hanging from the tree. Had she done that?

Cai and Hannah were standing below the dangling end of the branch. Not wanting to be left out, Antonia hurried after them. Cai had cleared a path, snapping off the smaller branches blocking their way. They positioned themselves round the half-hacked branch.

"On the count of three," said Cai. "One, two, three!"

Antonia pushed the branch up. It was

stronger than she thought. The sinewy wood refused to snap.

"Twist!" commanded Cai.

They twisted the branch clockwise then anticlockwise. They rocked it up and down like a seesaw until finally it began to creak.

"Keep going!" called Cai encouragingly.

Antonia tried harder. The seal gave another weak cry, spurring her on. With a superhuman effort, they wrenched the branch this way and that until, with a satisfying crack, it broke.

"Steady," said Hannah as they guided it to the ground and pulled it clear of the tree. Antonia immediately set about freeing the seal from the smaller branches still penning her in.

The seal groaned. Her body shuddered then

lay very still. Something about the seal's shudder worried Antonia. Gently she prodded her in the side. Nothing, not even the slightest twitch of a muscle. Even before Cai cleared the twigs from round her head to reveal the seal's cloudy eyes, Antonia knew there was nothing she could do. They were too late. The seal was dead.

Trembling with the effort not to cry, Antonia moved away to help the other seals on the beach.

"What was that?" asked Hannah sharply.

Antonia paused. She'd heard it too, a weak, kitten-like cry. She raced back to the tree. It was coming from the dead seal. Antonia groped beneath its stiff body until her fingers brushed against something warm and alive.

Carefully she drew the seal pup out from under her mother. She was so tiny. Antonia guessed she was only a week or so old. She was trembling with fear, but apart from that she seemed unharmed.

"That's amazing!" Hannah exclaimed.

"Steady," crooned Antonia. "You're safe now."

Anxiously the seal pushed her nose at Antonia's hand and made a funny snuffling sound. Her whiskers tickled, making Antonia laugh for the first time since she'd arrived on the beach. Their efforts hadn't been totally in vain.

"You poor little thing. I bet you're hungry."

Antonia removed her coat and jumper, wrapped the seal inside her jumper then put her coat back on.

"Well done," said Cai. "She's too young to leave on her own, isn't she? We'll have to take her back with us. She'll be Ocean Watch's first marine animal."

If Kathleen gets here in time. Where is she? Antonia stared up at the broken cliffs as if she might see Kathleen scaling down them on a rope.

"We have to get on." Cai set out across the beach. "There isn't time to stand around."

Antonia made a rough pen for the seal pup with broken tree branches. The pup seemed content to doze. Antonia was exhausted too, but there was so much more to do. Slowly she moved around the beach, checking the rest of the seals. As far as she could see, none of them were seriously injured, but a few had

cuts and scratches that would need treatment. Antonia hoped Kathleen remembered to bring medical supplies with her. Thankfully a good antiseptic would be enough to heal these seals because her magic was completely worn out.

Antonia bent over a plump seal with a cut near his flipper. "You're all right," she said, stroking his face. "We'll soon fix you up."

"Hooray!" cried Cai suddenly.

"What is it?" called Hannah.

"It's Kathleen!"

Antonia had been vaguely aware of a buzzing sound and now she realised why. A motorboat was heading for the beach.

"Who's that behind her?" she asked.

"Pardon?" said Cai. He squinted out to sea. "You're right. There are two boats. The second

one has a man in it. Do you know him, Hannah?"

Hannah shook her head. "I've never seen him before in my life," she said.

"Doesn't matter who he is," said Antonia cheerfully. "He's just what we need. More hands. Come on. Let's wade out and help them."

Chapter Fifteen

"Well done, everyone," said Kathleen as she waded ashore. "I knew you were sensible enough to leave on your own while I went back for help." She winked at Antonia, Cai and Hannah. "This is my neighbour, Ben. You met his wife, Jane, and their baby son yesterday."

Antonia stared at Ben in astonishment. Wasn't Jane the one who'd tried to close them down? Why had Kathleen brought him along to help?

They pulled the boats up on the beach while Kathleen inspected the cliffs to make sure there was no danger from a further landslide.

"The cliffs looked sturdy when I left the children here to get help," she told Ben, "but I thought I'd check again."

Ashen-faced, Ben unloaded the supplies: shovels, a saw and medical equipment including bandages and antiseptic.

"I can't believe this has happened," he kept repeating. "I was on my way here to fish when Kathleen asked me to help. It's a very special place. I love watching the seals."

Once everything had been unloaded, Antonia showed Kathleen the seal pup.

"Her mother didn't survive." She swallowed then added, "She needs feeding."

"That changes things slightly," said Kathleen. "Someone needs to take you back to Ocean Watch. Ben, would you mind? The seals need treating before we do anything else."

"No problem."

Kathleen delved into her coat pocket and pulled out a wooden dolphin key ring with several keys dangling from it. "Go in through the utility room. It's the gold key. There's powdered milk in the cupboard under the sink. It's easy to make up. The instructions are on the tin. When the seal's finished, put her in a cage in the lounge. The shed still smells of paint."

Antonia was longing to feed the seal pup, but thought she might be more use if she stayed to help with the injured seals.

"Wouldn't it be better if Hannah went instead of me?" she asked. "She knows where everything is."

Kathleen stared at Antonia kindly. "You look exhausted, my dear. I suspect you've been working much harder than you realise. Go and feed the pup, and if by that time you're feeling better, Ben can wait for you and bring you back."

"Thanks." Antonia felt grateful and guilty at the same time.

Ben told Antonia to put the seal in the locker at the front of the boat and leave the door open.

"The sea is still quite choppy. She'll be safer in there," he explained.

Antonia didn't mind. It would have been nice to cuddle the seal pup, but wild animals weren't pets. It was best to handle them as little as possible.

To her embarrassment, Antonia fell asleep on the boat ride home. One minute she was sitting on the wooden bench with the wind in her hair, and the next she was waking up sprawled along the bench with her face pressed into its wooden slats. Antonia wiped away the dribble trickling from her mouth before she sat up.

Ben grinned. "Got up early?" he commented. "Kathleen said the coastguard woke her by ringing to tell her about the landslide."

"It was very early," agreed Antonia. "And we didn't have time for breakfast." Her stomach grumbled as if backing her up.

"While you're feeding the pup, I'll nip home and make some sandwiches and a Thermos flask of tea to take back with us. How does that sound?"

"Brilliant," said Antonia.

At Kathleen's, Antonia put the baby seal into a cage while she made up a bottle of milk. It felt funny being in Kathleen's house alone. Antonia realised she was tiptoeing as she moved around the utility room.

"Thank goodness Kathleen thought to get this in," she said as she made up the powdered milk and poured it into a sterilised bottle. She put on a pair of disposable gloves and took

it to the lounge. She was just going to get the seal from the cage when the doorbell rang.

Antonia's first thought was to ignore it. Her mum had taught her never to answer the door when she was alone in the house. But of course it would only be Ben coming back with the sandwiches and tea. Leaving the bottle of milk on the table, Antonia went to the door. It wasn't until she opened it that she realised her mistake. Two people stood on the doorstep, a smartly dressed young woman and an older man with glasses. A cold feeling crept over Antonia, freezing her to the spot.

"Good morning, I'm Susan Birch, and this is my colleague Brian Masters from West Wood Council. We've an appointment with your grandmother."

Antonia stared at Susan blankly. Why did they want to see her grandmother?

"It's about the planning permission," prompted Susan.

Antonia swallowed, hoping Susan couldn't hear her heart thudding against her chest. She meant *Kathleen*!

"Mrs Abbot's not here," she stammered. "There's been a landslide. She's out saving seals."

"Oh!" said Susan, startled. "I hope it's not serious. Erm, we were hoping for a look around. Not that it matters. I only came back with my colleague because he's interested in what Mrs Abbot's doing here. I could have rung her with the news, but never mind."

She stared at Antonia, suddenly taking in her

bedraggled appearance, then took a discreet step back. "Can you pass on a message? Please tell Mrs Abbot that she doesn't need council permission to run her charity from home. Not unless she's going to be employing people or she's going to extend the property in any way."

"And can you give her this?" Brian Masters held out a card. "It's got my mobile number and my email address on it. If Mrs Abbot is looking for volunteers then I'd be interested."

"Really? That's great news. Thank you." In a daze, Antonia took the card and put it on the table by the front door.

She waved goodbye then hurried back to the seal pup. On her way, Antonia shouted with joy.

It was OK! Ocean Watch was allowed to go

ahead. And the man from the council wanted to be a volunteer! Antonia couldn't stop smiling as the baby seal hungrily sucked from the bottle.

Chapter Sixteen

Antonia fed the seal pup, wiping milk from her whiskery face before returning her to the cage. Then she rang Hannah's mum and explained where they were.

"Sounds like your last day's going to be a busy one," said Mrs Davies.

Antonia stared at the phone in surprise. She'd forgotten it was their last day.

"Don't worry. You can stay as late as you like. Ring me when you've finished and I'll come and pick you up," said Mrs Davies.

Ben returned, carrying an enormous picnic bag. "Jane helped," he said. "I believe there was a slight misunderstanding between her and Kathleen yesterday. She tells me she wasn't very polite. She had this funny idea that Kathleen was starting some kind of zoo. She's been very protective since Matty was born. Now I've explained Ocean Watch to her she's much happier. She says she owes you all an apology."

Antonia's heart swooped like a bird. She could hardly believe that everything was going

right for a change. She couldn't wait to return to the seals' beach and tell everyone the good news.

"Are you sure you're up for this?" asked Ben kindly. "You looked whacked. Jane says you can go round to ours."

"Like this?" Antonia couldn't help laughing. She knew she was a state. She was covered in scratches, her hair was tangled and she was filthy dirty.

Ben laughed too. "It might be a good idea to have a wash first," he suggested.

"'Thanks," said Antonia. "But I'm coming back with you. I wouldn't be able to settle here when there's so much work to be done."

"Me neither," said Ben.

By the time they returned to the seals'

beach, Kathleen and Hannah had treated all of the injured seals.

"There are lots of pups," said Hannah. "They seem to have recovered the quickest. Kathleen said we'll need to check up on them over the next week just to make sure though."

Ben pulled a blanket from his bag and spread it on the ground. "A late breakfast or is it an early lunch?"

"Brunch," said Cai, who had a word for everything that involved food.

Ben unpacked the bag while Antonia told everyone about the visit from the council, and Brian Masters wanting to become a volunteer. Then Ben apologised for Jane's behaviour the previous day and asked if Kathleen could

forgive her enough to let him become an Ocean Watch volunteer too.

"I never say no to help," said Kathleen, beaming at him.

Antonia's heart soared. Now Kathleen and Hannah had two volunteers. They'd definitely need them with her and Cai going home tomorrow! Thank goodness they'd got Ocean Watch ready in time. There was lots of room for any injured animals now.

After that the picnic brunch felt more like a party. The seals, crowded up at one end of the beach, watched them. One or two of the braver ones ventured over. They were slow and cumbersome as they hauled themselves across the sand to sniff inquisitively at the picnic bag. It was tempting to throw them a

crust, but everyone knew better than to do that.

The rest of the morning was spent cutting up the tree.

"I'll pick up the larger pieces in the car," said Kathleen. "It wouldn't be practical to take them back in the boat."

At midday Kathleen called a halt to the work. "Enough," she said. "You children look exhausted."

They pushed the boats out to sea and climbed aboard. Antonia and Cai went with Ben, and Hannah went with Kathleen. As they sailed out to sea, Antonia saw four dark specks racing towards them. She held her breath.

Was it? Yes, it was! The specks grew larger and turned into dolphins – Vision, Dancer, Lulu

and Rolly. Their silver bodies flashed in the weak autumn sunlight as they swam nearer.

"Look!" cried Ben. "Dolphins!"

Vision and the other dolphins gave piercing whistles of thanks as they swam by.

Thank you, Antonia answered in her head. She would miss Vision and his family. But hopefully they'd meet again when she came back to visit Hannah, Kathleen and Ocean Watch!

"Get that!" Ben was so excited he nearly fell out of the boat. "Did you hear them whistle? I swear they were talking to us."

Antonia and Cai shared a smile.

"You know," said Cai, "I think they probably were!"

Buy more great Silver Dolphins books from HarperCollins at 10% off recommended retail price. FREE postage and packing in the UK.

Out Now:

Silver Dolphins – The Magic Charm	ISBN: 978-0-00-730968-9
Silver Dolphins – Secret Friends	ISBN: 978-0-00-730969-6
Silver Dolphins – Stolen Treasures	ISBN: 978-0-00-730970-2
Silver Dolphins – Double Danger	ISBN: 978-0-00-730971-9
Silver Dolphins – Broken Promises	ISBN: 978-0-00-730972-6
Silver Dolphins – Moonlight Magic	ISBN: 978-0-00-730973-3
Silver Dolphins – Rising Star	ISBN: 978-0-00-734812-1
Silver Dolphins – Stormy Skies	ISBN: 978-0-00-734813-8

All priced at £4.99

To purchase by Visa/Mastercard/Switch simply call
08707871724 or fax on **08707871725**

To pay by cheque, send a copy of this form with a cheque made payable to 'HarperCollins Publishers' to: Mail Order Dept. (Ref: BOB4), HarperCollins Publishers, Westerhill Road, Bishopbriggs, G64 2QT, making sure to include your full name, postal address and phone number.

From time to time HarperCollins may wish to use your personal data to send you details of other HarperCollins publications and offers. If you wish to receive information on other HarperCollins publications and offers please tick this box ☐

Do not send cash or currency. Prices correct at time of press.
Prices and availability are subject to change without notice.
Delivery overseas and to Ireland incurs a £2 per book postage and packing charge.